ROB CHILDS

COUNTY CUP

Book Seven
THE FINAL

Cup Winners

Illustrated by Robin Lawrie

CORGI YEARLING BOOKS

COUNTY CUP 7 : CUP WINNERS
A CORGI YEARLING BOOK : 0 440 863899

First publication in Great Britain

PRINTING HISTORY
Corgi Yearling edition published 2000

J91,901
£3·99

Set in 12/15 pt New Century Schoolbook by
Phoenix Typesetting, Ilkley, West Yorkshire

Corgi Yearling Books are published by Transworld Publishers,
61–63 Uxbridge Road, London W5 5SA,
a division of The Random House Group Ltd,
in Australia by Random House Australia (Pty) Ltd,
20 Alfred Street, Milsons Point, Sydney, NSW 2061, Australia,
in New Zealand by Random House New Zealand Ltd,
18 Poland Road, Glenfield, Auckland 10, New Zealand
and in South Africa by Random House (Pty) Ltd,
Endulini, 5a Jubilee Road, Parktown 2193, South Africa.

Made and printed in Great Britain by
Cox & Wyman Ltd, Reading, Berkshire

INTRODUCTION

Long ago, the historic county of Medland was made up of four separate regions. These divisions can now only be found on ancient maps, but people living in the old North, South, East and West Quarters remain loyal to their own area.

One example of how the traditional rivalry still survives is the County Cup soccer tournament for schools. Group games were played at first to find the Quarter Champions, who then clashed in the two-legged semi-finals. Now the stage is set – almost – for the County Final, the biggest match of the young footballers' lives.

The eventual Cup Winners will receive the much-prized silver trophy and be crowned as the new County Champions – the top team in Medland.

THE COUNTY OF MEDLAND

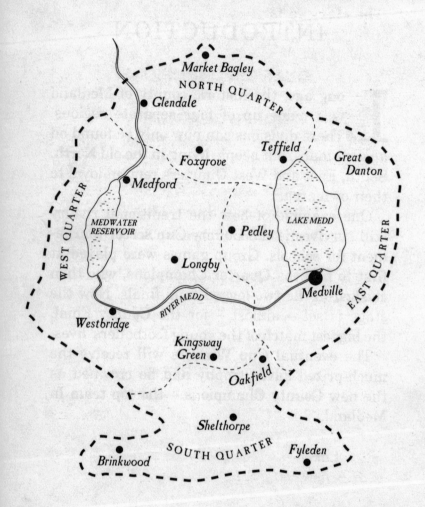

Market Bagley

NORTH QUARTER

Glendale

Teffield

Great Danton

Foxgrove

Medford

LAKE MEDD

WEST QUARTER

MEDWATER RESERVOIR

Pedley

Longby

EAST QUARTER

Medville

RIVER MEDD

Westbridge

Kingsway Green

Oakfield

Shelthorpe

SOUTH QUARTER

Fyleden

Brinkwood

CUP TRAIL

The story so far . . .

QUARTER CHAMPIONS

NORTH QUARTER
Glendale Community School

EAST QUARTER (Joint)
Lakeview High School, Medville

Medville Comprehensive School

SOUTH QUARTER
St Wystan's Comprehensive
School, Brinkwood

WEST QUARTER
Westbridge Community College

Note: Lakeview beat Medville in a play-off to qualify for semi-finals

GROUP TABLES

North Quarter

	P	W	D	L	F	A	Pts
Glendale	**3**	**2**	**1**	**0**	**9**	**5**	**7**
Foxgrove	3	2	0	1	8	3	6
Mkt Bagley	3	0	2	1	3	6	2
Teffield	3	0	1	2	4	10	1

East Quarter

	P	W	D	L	F	A	Pts
Lakeview	**3**	**1**	**2**	**0**	**5**	**3**	**5**
Medville	**3**	**1**	**2**	**0**	**5**	**3**	**5**
Needham	3	1	0	2	3	6	3
Gt Danton	3	0	2	1	2	3	2

South Quarter

	P	W	D	L	F	A	Pts
St Wystan's	**3**	**2**	**0**	**1**	**7**	**4**	**6**
Shelthorpe	3	2	0	1	7	5	6
Oakfield	3	1	0	2	9	8	3
Fyleden	3	1	0	2	3	9	3

West Quarter

	P	W	D	L	F	A	Pts
Westbridge	**3**	**2**	**1**	**0**	**7**	**4**	**7**
Riverside	3	1	2	0	8	7	5
Hillcrest	3	0	2	1	5	7	2
Kingsway Gn	3	0	1	2	4	6	1

SEMI-FINALS

SOUTH v EAST   ST WYSTAN'S v LAKEVIEW

Result: Lakeview won 3-2 on aggregate

WEST v NORTH   WESTBRIDGE v GLENDALE

Result: Teams level 4-4 on aggregate

Note: Westbridge and Glendale must now meet again in a play-off to decide which school will meet Lakeview in the Final.

. . . let's replay the highlights of these semi-finals first before meeting the teams and then enjoying the exciting climax to the County Cup . . .

9

SEMI-FINAL HIGHLIGHTS

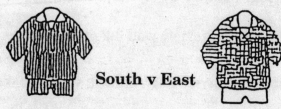

South v East

1st leg – St Wystan's 0 – 1 Lakeview

. . . 'There's likely to be a hard frost overnight,' Miss Jackson warned her Lakeview squad, 'but good footballers need to be prepared to play in all kinds of conditions.'

***

. . . The fact that the score remained 0–0 at half-time was due partly to the difficult conditions, but mostly to the outstanding form of the two goalkeepers.

***

. . . After a Saints' effort had been disallowed for offside, Lakeview scored from a corner. Harry drew back his left foot and connected sweetly, driving the ball low through a mass of bodies into the net for the winning goal.

2nd leg – Lakeview 2 – 2 St Wystan's

. . . 'Trust Elvis to get injured,' muttered Joe, the Lakeview wing-back. 'Who's gonna play in goal now?'

***

. . . *Soon after the kick-off, Lakeview's nervous new keeper seemed rooted to his line, as if stuck in the mud, and the Saints' number ten hooked the ball high into the roof of the net.*

***

. . . 'We'll have the wind and rain in our favour second half,' stressed Ben, the Lakeview captain, as his team trailed 2–1 at the interval. 'It's gonna be the Saints' turn to struggle now.'

***

. . . *'Great save!' cried Elvis from behind the goal as his stand-in turned a shot round the post. 'I'd have been proud of that one.'*

***

. . . The ball spun tantalizingly in the mud between him and the Saints' keeper, but Lakeview's Henry Tudor stretched out a boot to poke the ball past him and it trickled over the line for the equalizer.

Lakeview won 3–2 on aggregate

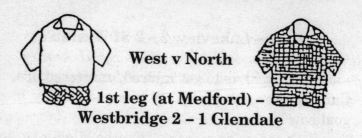

West v North

1st leg (at Medford) – Westbridge 2 – 1 Glendale

. . . The postponement of the first leg due to a frozen pitch meant that Westbridge would be at full strength for the re-match – Yagnesh would be back from India.

***

. . . *Yagnesh was unmarked and unhurried – and his shot was unstoppable.*

***

. . . Yagnesh struck again in the second half, dummying inside the full-back and curling his left-footed shot wide of the advancing goalie into the far corner of the net. It proved to be the winning goal.

***

2nd leg – Glendale 3 – 2 Westbridge

. . . Glendale took the lead early on when Robbie Jones overlapped up the right wing and whipped across a centre that Giant met with a full-length, diving header at the near post.

. . . After conceding two goals just before half-time, a shell-shocked Glendale could hardly believe they were now 2–1 behind and losing 4–2 on aggregate.

***

. . . Both teams brought on their hard men as second-half substitutes. 'I'm gonna get my retaliation in first before that nutter clobbers me,' scowled College's Dan Cross.

***

. . . After Dan had fouled him, the red mist came down over Carl's eyes. He ploughed into Dan like a runaway truck and they were soon brawling in the penalty area mud. The two subs were sent off for violent conduct.

***

. . . The spot-kick flew past the College post – the right side for the keeper, the wrong side for the kicker.

***

. . . Westbridge then suffered a late double whammy. Having been coasting into the Cup Final, the wheels of the College bandwagon had suddenly fallen off.

Teams level 4 – 4 on aggregate: play-off required

LAKEVIEW HIGH SCHOOL

Medium-sized secondary school in the county town of Medville in the East Quarter. Pupils in year groups 7, 8 and 9 only, aged between 11 and 14.

Headteacher: *Mr John Underwood*
P.E. teacher: *Miss Ruth Jackson*
School colours: *blue shirts, white shorts and socks*
Year 7 soccer captain: *Ben Thorpe*
Usual team formation: *3–5–2, using wing-backs*

Year 7 soccer squad

(Elvis)
Michael King

James Black Andy Peacock Harry Glenn

Joe Vernon Steve Jarvis Ben Thorpe Ian Coates Dan Maynard

(Henry)
Matthew Tudor Jaspal Singh

plus: Gary (Gordon) Bennett, Manjit Bedi, Will Freeman, Thomas Farr, Alan Davis, Nathan Finch

CAPTAIN'S Notes...

Well, who'd have thought it? Here we are in the final of the County Cup! Back in September, as nervous new kids at Lakeview High, we were totally gob-smacked to learn that our coach was a woman. But we soon found out that Miss Jackson knows all about the game — and plays it better than any of us lot too. She's just won her first cap for England!

We're in pretty good form as well, though, and haven't lost a game yet this term. Mind you, we came close against the Saints when an injury to Elvis, our keeper, nearly cost us the semi-final. We could just do with scoring a few more goals. Don't think we've notched more than two in a game since Ravi Mistry left before Christmas. Perhaps we're saving up the Big Win for the final itself! Hope so.

I said in my original notes that it should be an interesting season. Well, I was wrong — it's been amazing!

GLENDALE COMMUNITY SCHOOL

L arge comprehensive school in market town of Glendale in the North Quarter.

Headteacher: *Mrs Margaret Burrows*
Head of P.E. Dept: *Mr Brian Fisher*
School colours: *royal blue shirts, shorts and socks*
Year 7 soccer captain: *Paul Stevens*
Usual team formation: *4–2–4*

Year 7 soccer squad

(Crackers)
Ian Jacobs

(Batty)   (Dips)
Robbie Jones Paul Stevens Tom Bateman Dipesh Patel

(Wainy)
Hanif Khan   Alex Wainwright

(Giant)   (Leggy)
Nick Green Harry Taylor Chris Kemp Tim Lamb

plus: Scott Harris, Jeff Smith, David Nash, Richard Curtis, Gary Thomas, Carl Simpson (suspended from Cup)

16

Brilliant! Our last gasp victory over Westbridge in the second leg gives us another chance in the play-off to reach the County Final. After such an escape even Mr Fisher reckons our name must be on the Cup this year! We intend to keep the engraver busy. We're already in the final of the North Quarter Cup against local rivals, the Foxes.

We're still banging in the goals left, right and centre — literally. Our twin strikers, Giant and Kempy, plus wingers Nick and Leggy, have scored over 60 goals between them. The bad news, I'm afraid, is that we're still leaking too many goals at the back.

At least the Destroyer, Carl Simpson, can't go and mess things up for us any more in the County Cup. His two-match ban for getting sent off in the semi means he misses the rest of that competition.

Anyway, you can count on one thing for sure with us as we go all out for the Cup Double — plenty of goalmouth action!

Large comprehensive school in the town of Westbridge on the River Medd in the West Quarter.

Headteacher: *Mr Walter Hooper*
P.E. teacher: *Mr Doug Griffiths*
School colours: *white shirts, black shorts and socks*
Year 7 soccer captain: *Emerson Marshall*
Usual team formation: *4–1–3–2 (attacking sweeper system)*

Year 7 soccer squad:

Adam Trent

Eddie Atkins   Emerson Marshall   Brad Gibson   Craig Dalton

(Kenny)
William Kennedy

(King Kong)
Richard Congdon   Sam Lucas   Yagnesh Sharma

(Bax)
Iain Baxter   Oliver Yates

plus: Mark Palmer, Ajay Jethwa, Jacob Roberts, (Bob) Dylan Small, Jim Chalmers, Dean Matthews, Andy Thornton, Dan Cross (suspended from Cup)

Typical! Just when the College's damaged soccer pitches are almost ready for action at last, it's nearly the end of the season. It'll be great to play the last couple of league games at home to clinch the West Quarter Championship, but it won't make any difference to the County Cup. The semi-final play-off is in Medford again – where we won the first leg – and then the Final will be staged on a neutral ground.

So the 'Westbridge Wanderers' are still on our travels, despite the wrong turning we took into the Glendale cul-de-sac. We've now got over the shock of that late defeat when we thought we were already in the Final. Mr Griffiths accused us of being over-confident, but we won't make the same mistake of throwing it away again.

Be warned, Glendale – even if the suspended Dan Cross can't get you now, then Big Ollie and the rest of us will. We're out for revenge!

Lakeview

Lying third in the East Quarter league – with Medville Comp having already clinched the title. Made an early exit from the local cup, but unbeaten so far this term. Finding goalscoring a problem since the departure of Ravi Mistry.

Leading goalscorers: Tudor – 11, Mistry – 8, Thorpe – 7, Singh – 6
County Cup goalscorers: Mistry – 2, Tudor – 2, Thorpe – 2, Vernon – 1, Singh – 1, Glenn – 1, Peacock – 1

Glendale

A free-scoring team, but trailing well behind leaders Foxgrove in the North Quarter league. Hoping to pull off a Cup Double instead, with the Foxes also their opponents in the Final of the local cup.

Leading goalscorers: Taylor – 26, Kemp – 17, Green – 12, Lamb – 7
County Cup goalscorers: Taylor – 4, Kemp – 4, Green – 2, Khan – 1, Patel – 1, Simpson – 1

Westbridge

Knocked out of the local cup competition, but aiming to do the Big Double – winning both the Championship and the County Cup. Now top of the West Quarter league table, two points clear of rivals Riverside.

Leading goalscorers: Baxter – 13, Lucas – 11, Sharma – 9, Yates – 9
County Cup goalscorers: Sharma – 4, Baxter – 2, Yates – 2, Lucas – 1, Congdon – 1, Small – 1

. . . OK, all set for the Final? Well, not quite. There's that semi-final play-off to sort out first between Glendale and Westbridge to decide who will meet Lakeview. Wonder which school you might be supporting? . . .

QUARTER CUP

. . . there's just five minutes to go and with the scores level at two goals each, the North Quarter trophy is still up for grabs . . .

'Corner!' chorused the Glendale players and supporters in unison.

'C'mon, Blues, let's make this one count,' shouted Paul Stevens, the captain. 'We've had enough chances.'

A few seconds later, they had another. The corner was only half-cleared and the ball fell invitingly at the feet of the Blues' substitute who was lurking just outside the area. Time seemed to freeze, as if wanting to capture the moment that the cup was won.

The spiky-haired number thirteen drew back his left boot and then unleashed a shot of terrific power, breaking the spell. It might have broken a window too. The ball soared high and wide of the goal and slammed into the metal grille that protected a classroom window behind the pitch.

Carl Simpson could hardly believe that he'd missed. He'd dreamt last night of scoring the winning goal and ending up as the big hero.

'What a waste of space!'

Carl whirled round at the taunt and fixed his glare on little Alex Wainwright. 'I'll *do* you for that,' he thundered.

Wainy brushed aside the threat. 'I don't think so,' he retorted. 'You're already in enough trouble as it is.'

Carl scowled, knowing that Wainy was right. On top of his behaviour problems at school, there had now been a home visit from a social worker to investigate suspicions of abuse by his father. Carl's back and stomach were a mass of scratches and ugly bruises.

Paul clapped his hands to urge his teammates on. 'C'mon, keep it going, Blues!' he cried. 'One's bound to go in soon. We're all over 'em.'

In reality, their North Quarter rivals Foxgrove had missed just as many chances to settle the match, but the Foxes' hopes of a league and cup double were about to be dashed.

Paul won the aerial duel for the goal-kick and the ball found its way out to the Blues' lanky left-winger. Leggy strode past his marker and curled a deep cross into the Foxes' penalty area smack on to the head of the number nine, Harry Taylor – and heads at this age didn't come any higher than Giant's.

Glendale's leading scorer tumbled to the ground without seeing where the ball had gone. The Foxes keeper had a good view, though. All he could do was watch the guided missile fly well beyond his reach and drop just underneath the crossbar into the far corner of the net.

'The winner!' yelled Wainy.

The excited forecast may have been premature, but at least it proved accurate. Shortly afterwards, as Paul stepped forward to receive the Quarter Cup, Giant let out a great whoop behind him.

'One down, one to go!'

The captain smiled modestly as he held up the trophy to the cheers of the Glendale fans. 'Yeah, but the next one is The Big One,' Paul murmured to himself. 'The County Cup!'

. . . only one of the winners was not looking forward to the County Cup play-off against Westbridge – Carl Simpson was now banned from the competition after his sending off in the second leg of the semi-final . . .

AT LAKEVIEW

. . . meanwhile, over in the east of Medland, Miss Jackson is using part of a practice session to assess the form and fitness of the two goalkeepers in her Year 7 soccer squad . . .

'How's the shoulder feeling, Michael?' asked the teacher.

'OK now, miss,' the chubby, first-choice goalie assured her. 'It's fully fit again. Can't feel a thing.'

Miss Jackson knew how much the boy was desperate to be back in the team after the injury that caused him to miss the second leg of their Cup semi-final. 'Glad to hear it,' she said. 'But there's no need to go throwing yourself about all over the place to try and impress me. I already know how brilliant you are.'

Michael King reddened with embarassment as he saw the teacher smiling at him. Perhaps he *had* been overdoing the acrobatics a little.

'Anyway, take a break now so I can watch Gary in action,' Miss Jackson continued. 'He's not been much more than a ball-boy behind the goal since we started.'

'Played, Elvis,' said Gary Bennett generously as they swapped over. 'You made some wicked stops there.'

'Cheers, Gordon,' Elvis replied, using his pal's nickname too. 'Got to prove to Jacko I'm worth my place in the side again after the way you played last week.'

'Most of them saves were down to luck.'

Gary was being too modest. It was thanks to his heroics in goal that Lakeview had avoided their first league defeat since Christmas by scraping a 1–1 draw. Elvis had to acknowledge, if only to himself, that his one-time understudy had become a serious rival.

Miss Jackson was using this part of the session not only to cast her eye over the two keepers, but also to give the team's strikers and midfield players some much-needed shooting practice. They were all well aware that Ravi Mistry was still their second highest scorer behind 'Henry' Tudor – and Ravi had left Lakeview four months ago.

Elvis was kept almost as busy as when he'd been in goal, only it involved more legwork in chasing after the stray shots.

'C'mon, get 'em on target,' he bellowed crossly, returning from another trip to the hedge. 'I'm working harder than Gordon.'

When Henry connected sweetly at last, Gary was well positioned to dive to his right and push the ball round the post.

'Great stuff, Gordon!' Henry cried to mask his disappointment at not scoring.

'That was one of my specials. Elvis wouldn't have got near it.'

'Watch it!' Elvis called out. 'I heard that.'

'You were meant to,' Henry laughed, knowing the jibe would provoke such a response from his mate. 'Bet that's all you would've done with that shot – watched it go in!'

At the other end of the pitch, the rest of the squad were working in pairs, taking it in turns to run with the ball at each other. Cousins Joe and Harry had formed a very competitive partnership.

CRUNCH!

As Joe tried to fool Harry with what he hoped was a clever shimmy and sidestep, the full-back timed his tackle to perfection. Harry went in hard with a block and came away with the ball, leaving Joe on his backside. Harry dribbled the ball off, giggling to himself, and wasn't prepared for Joe's quick recovery and chase.

Harry sensed the danger too late. Joe slid in from the side to stretch out a long leg and hook the ball away off his cousin's toes, sending Harry sprawling to the ground in the process. They both sat up, breathing hard, and then grinned at each other.

'Anything you can do . . .' Joe laughed.

'. . . I can do better!' Harry finished off for him. 'I'm still winning – I've got in more successful tackles than you.'

Joe shrugged. 'Lost count. Anyway, you're more of a defender than I am. That's why I play wing-back so I can go forward to support the attack every chance I get – just like Jacko does herself.'

They gazed back down the pitch to where their coach was demonstrating some shooting technique. Miss Jackson tapped the ball forward then drilled it low past Gary into the bottom corner of the net.

Harry chuckled. 'Well, if she's feeling nervous about Saturday, she's sure not letting it show.'

'She's bound to be – I mean, wouldn't you?' said Joe, shaking his head in wonder. 'Just imagine – getting picked to play for England!'

*. . . check back to the end of Book 5, **CUP GLORY**, for details of Jacko's international debut, but read on to find out more about the two cousins . . .*

FLOODLIGHT FOCUS

... on **Joe Vernon**

school	Lakeview
other teams	East Quarter
	Medville Majors (Sunday League)
position	wing-back
best foot forward	right
age	12
build	average
nickname	J. V.
ambition	to be a millionaire!
pets	mice & a rabbit
family	kid sister
superstitions	lucky colour blue
hobbies	TV & football
so embarrassing!	giving away a penalty

favourites

school subject	Games
football team	Manchester United
book	joke books
TV programme	Tom & Jerry cartoons
music	pop
food	fish & chips
drink	orange squash
word/saying	Shoot!

FLOODLIGHT FOCUS

. . . on **Harry Glenn**

school	Lakeview (ex-Medville Comp)
other teams	none
position	defender
best foot forward	left
age	11, nearly 12
build	short
nickname	Glenn (by Comp kids)
ambition	to be a teacher (!)
pets	cat
family	no brothers or sisters
superstitions	it's bad luck to meet old Comp kids
hobbies	computers, reading
so embarrassing!	scoring an own goal

favourites

school subject	history
football team	England
book	any about kings & queens
TV programme	any history programme
music	instrumentals
food	cheese & pickle sandwiches
drink	milk
word/saying	I don't believe it!

PLAY-OFF PREPARATIONS

. . . let's see how the soccer squads of Westbridge and Glendale are preparing for their own big match – the semi-final play-off in the County Cup . . .

AT WESTBRIDGE

'Yes!' cried Bax as the ball smacked into the netting. 'No trouble!'

The sprawling goalkeeper cursed silently and then clambered back on to his feet. 'Huh!' Adam grunted, unable to resist a taunt to seek a little revenge. 'Pity you couldn't do that when it mattered to save us all this bother with the play-off.'

Everyone knew that his crucial penalty miss in the second leg was a very touchy subject with Iain Baxter. You had to be either big or brave to cheek him over it – and Adam was both.

Oliver Yates was the next kicker 'on the spot'. He was Bax's main rival for the role of penalty-taker in the side and was keen to impress the approaching teacher. He settled the ball carefully on the white blob of paint and took six long paces back.

'C'mon, Ollie, hurry up, will you,' cried Emerson from the queue of players waiting for their turn. 'We're freezing here, standing about.'

There was no rushing Oliver. He looked up to catch the goalie's eye, gave him a broad grin and then loped forward. Anyone who didn't know Adam might have accused him of diving out of the way of the rocket, but he had simply guessed wrongly. He went to the right, the ball sped to his left and both ended up in the back of the net.

'Try not to commit yourself too early, Adam,' Mr Griffiths called out. 'Stay on your feet a fraction longer and you might give yourself a better chance of making the save.'

Adam could hear Bax sniggering in the queue and increased the level of his concentration. Only one of the next four penalties was put past him. His best save came when he plucked Emerson's effort out of the air at full stretch, earning himself high praise from the captain.

'Total respect, man!' Emerson grinnned. 'I hit that one real well.'

Bax sauntered casually forward again to position the ball. 'OK, then, Adam,' he smirked.

'Which way is this one gonna go, eh? Any idea?'

'Not yet,' Adam replied honestly. 'But I will do when you hit it.'

'Doubt it.'

'Just get on with it, will yer.'

Bax did a little jink in his run-up to try and put the keeper off and then struck the ball with the side of his right boot, placing it low to Adam's left. The keeper hurled himself full length and – to his relief – saw the ball heading in the same direction. He even clung on to it with both hands and immediately stood up to brandish the ball in the air in triumph as Bax sank to his knees.

'Yes, yes, very good, Adam,' said Mr Griffiths, unaware of the extra edge given to the duel. 'Well saved, but this isn't the World Cup Final, you know. Just a bit of penalty practice – which it looks like you need, Iain.'

'Looks like Big Ollie might take over your job, Bax,' Adam teased him.

'No way!' Bax retorted. 'I'm still the penalty king round here.'

Adam laughed. 'I reckon you might just have lost your throne.'

'We'll see about that,' Bax muttered under his breath.

AT GLENDALE

The Glendale squad was also practising their skills at finding the net – or at least half of them were. The other half were trying just as hard to keep the ball out of it. The boys were enjoying their favourite game of attack versus defence – and the attackers were winning as usual.

'Remind us what the score is, captain,' smirked Chris Kemp after his shot scraped the bar to earn an extra point. 'I've lost count.'

Paul Stevens gave a shrug. 'Only about 16–4. We can soon put that right.'

Giant let out a guffaw. 'This boy never knows when he's beat.'

'We're never beat,' Paul replied defiantly and then grinned. 'Just sometimes the other team score more than us, that's all.'

Paul backed up his words straight away by adding another point to the defence's tally with a long clearance over the halfway line. Leggy retrieved the ball and ambled along the left touchline, before whipping the ball across the field to his fellow winger, Nick Green.

The clever switch of play caught the defence wrong-footed. Nick accelerated past a limp attempt at a challenge, cut inside and let fly from about thirty metres. Crackers in goal wasn't

expecting a shot so soon, but he was well-positioned off his line and snatched the ball out of the air.

'Well held!' praised the teacher. 'One point for the shot.'

'But not three for a goal,' Crackers sniggered, rolling the ball out to his captain. 'Take it away, Stevo. Get it up into their half again.'

The defence managed to do so twice more before the attackers combined fluently to score the best goal of the session. Hanif Khan won the ball in midfield with a firm tackle and released Nick up the wing again with a defence-splitting pass. Nick resisted the temptation to go for glory himself this time and screwed the ball back low instead for the incoming Kempy to hit in his stride. Crackers' dive was in vain. His outstretched right hand flailed wildly at the ball as it hurtled by and buried itself in the corner of the net.

The scorer leapt up to slap Giant's raised palm in celebration. 'You and Leggy keep providing the ammunition,' Kempy shouted across to Nick, 'and me and Giant will keep pulling the trigger.'

'Right, lads, let's finish on that high note,' Mr Fisher called out. 'Gather round now.'

The players listened while their coach confirmed the team for the play-off and reminded them of what he expected. 'Let's play to our strengths,' he stressed. 'Use the wings and get plenty of crosses into the middle.'

Leggy raised his hand. 'Have Glendale ever won the County Cup, Mr Fisher?'

He shook his head. 'No, but there's a first time for everything,' he said with a smile and then made them all laugh with his next remark at the left-winger's expense. 'Including you getting your name on the scoresheet in this competition!'

. . . before the schools clash again to try and win a place in the Final, let's have a more in-depth look at what it takes to be the last line of defence . . .

ADVANCED GOALKEEPING SKILLS

The goalkeeper is a team's vital last line of defence. He needs sharp reflexes, concentration and courage – plus a thick skin and a loud voice!

Want to be one of these unsung superstars? Take a few tips from me.

✓ Be the boss of the box – tell teammates where to be, what to do and who to mark
✓ Catch the ball whenever possible – keep possession
✓ If you can't catch it, punch hard upwards or sideways, or palm the ball over the bar or round the post out of danger
✓ Low shots: get part of body behind hands as a second line of defence – spread fingers out, pointing down, little fingers almost touching
✓ High shots: take off from one foot to gain extra height – hands behind ball, fingers spread out, thumbs almost touching
✓ Body shots: chest height – get body in line with shot and bring it back to cushion impact, wrapping hands, arms and body behind ball

✓ Diving at feet; keep body level to ground to act as a long barrier. Timing of dive is vital. Wrap body around ball to protect it

✓ Throwing – find teammate with underarm roll, or shoulder throw with bent arm or even overarm throw with straight arm for longer distances

✓ Look the part – wear smart kit and have gloves and cap ready for use

✓ Keep practising

'KEEPER'S BALL!'

SEMI-FINAL: PLAY-OFF

WESTBRIDGE v GLENDALE

Saturday 14 March
k.o. 10 a.m.
Referee: Mr J. Riley

. . . the play-off is being staged at Riverside Comprehensive, Medford, where Westbridge won the first leg – it's half-time and the two schools are still tied . . .

'Pity you let them equalize just before the break, lads,' Mr Fisher told his Glendale team. 'They didn't deserve to score.'

Crackers glared round at his defenders. 'You gave that big kid a free header from the corner,' complained the keeper. 'I stood no chance.'

'My fault,' Paul Stevens admitted honestly. 'I was the one supposed to be marking him. He gave me the slip as the ball came over. Soz, guys.'

'That number nine's a handful for anybody,' said Mr Fisher, trying to make his captain feel better. 'But otherwise, he's hardly had a kick.'

'Bet he's had a few from Stevo!' Leggy put in, smirking.

Not even the equalizer had spoiled the winger's good mood. Tim Lamb had done exactly what the teacher wanted him to. He'd scored his first goal in the County Cup. In the football equivalent of a pinball machine, the ball had ricocheted among the threshing bodies in a goal-mouth scramble until he had managed to stretch out a leg – a very long leg – to poke it into the net.

'Better late than never, Tim,' Mr Fisher chuckled. 'Not exactly a thing of beauty, your goal, but they all count.'

Some distance away, the mood in the College camp was one of relief. The players knew they were fortunate to be on level terms.

'Magic header, Big Ollie!' enthused Kenny, their sweeper. 'A real bullet. The keeper never even made a move for it.'

'No sweat, man,' grinned the striker. 'Sam put the ball right on me bonce.'

'Can't miss a massive target like that,' chuckled Sam Lucas.

'So why aren't we finding it more often, then?' demanded Mr Griffiths.

When there was no reply, the teacher proceeded to give his players several reasons, sharing his criticism around the team. He left the boys in no doubt at all that he wasn't satisfied with their first-half performance and expected a great deal better from them in the second.

'We shouldn't even be here today,' he complained, reminding them of how they had allowed Glendale to score two late goals to force this play-off. 'So are you going to lie down and let this lot walk all over you – or are you going to prove you're worth your place in the Final?'

The teacher let his challenge dangle in the air for a few moments and then added simply, 'It's up to you. Show me what you're made of.'

It was the blue shirts of Glendale, however, that swept forward straight from the re-start. Wainy and Leggy linked up along the left, allowing the winger to send over a high cross into the penalty area. Giant managed to get his head to the ball – as always, it seemed – but made only glancing contact and keeper Adam Trent was able to turn the ball round a post.

'C'mon, skipper, get a grip on that kid,' Adam urged. 'He's winning everything in the air.'

There was little that Emerson could really say

in response. He was taller than average himself, but still had to look up to Giant. He concentrated on the task in hand now, the thankless one of trying to mark Giant and stop him winning the ball from the corner.

On this occasion, at least, Emerson succeeded. He timed his run a fraction better than his opponent and rose to meet the ball and flick it away out of danger. At a cost. There was a clash of heads in mid-air and both boys needed treatment before the game could continue.

As play swung briefly to the other end of the pitch, they caught each other's eye. 'You've got a hard nut,' grinned Emerson, dabbing at his cut ear with a swab of cotton wool.

'Look who's talking!' retorted Giant, pointing at his own forehead. 'I've got a lump coming up here as big as an egg.'

Emerson peered at the damage. 'Shouldn't try and head anything else if I were you,' he laughed. 'It'll hurt like crazy.'

'It'll be worth it,' Giant muttered. 'So long as I score.'

Giant didn't have too long to wait until he opened his account. Five minutes later, after a period of constant pressure on the Westbridge goal, Giant put Glendale 2–1 in front by the less painful means of his right boot. Hanif cleverly slipped a pass between two defenders into his teammate's ungainly stride and Giant did the rest with a fierce strike that took Adam by surprise.

It was another five minutes before the Glendale keeper was seriously troubled for the first time since the break. Apart from kicking clear the odd back-pass and catching a couple of crosses, Crackers had been largely idle, but he was ever watchful for any possible threat. He saw it coming before anybody else sensed the danger.

'Dips! Batty!' Crackers cried out. 'Cover that number nine.'

Oliver Yates had wandered over into space on the Westbridge left flank as Glendale attacked further upfield on that side of the pitch. Both full-back Robbie Jones and captain Paul had pushed forward in support without spotting the movement behind them. When the raid suddenly broke down, the ball was booted over their heads, and Oliver would have been in the clear if Batty hadn't been alerted to the situation.

Even so, he was not in a position to make an immediate challenge. Batty tried to jockey the powerful striker over towards the touchline to hold him up while reinforcements arrived, but Oliver had no intention of being herded into a cul-de-sac. He feinted to go down the line then suddenly cut inside, unbalancing Batty and leaving the defender on his backside.

Only Dipesh Patel now barred his path to goal, and even he wasn't ideally placed to do so. Dips saw the other striker galloping up in support through the middle and had the impossible task of attempting to cover both players. Two-against-one and he was the piggy caught in the middle.

'Yes, Ollie, to me!' cried Bax. 'I'm free.'

Oliver ignored his teammate at first, intent on

bustling past the defender and going for goal himself. But the repeated demands caused him to hesitate slightly and it was at that precise moment that Dips struck. Although he was much smaller and lighter than his opponent, Dips clattered into him and both of them crashed to the ground as the ball ran loose.

The referee almost blew for a foul but then called 'Play on!' as he saw the second white-shirted striker had a clear run at goal. Only Crackers now stood in Bax's way. Well, *stood* was perhaps not the correct word. Crackers was already charging out of his area towards him at full speed and Bax panicked. Instead of staying cool and dribbling past the keeper, Bax had a rush of blood and lobbed the ball over his head.

Everyone watched the flight of the ball with bated breath – including the winded Dips and Oliver. They watched it loop up, drop down, bounce and then bobble past the post for a goal-kick. Glendale remained 2–1 ahead.

By the time the teachers were summoned on to the pitch to attend to their own player, Dips was back on his feet. He was bending over, ruefully examining his right knee, but Oliver was still sitting and rubbing his ankle.

'Reckon I've twisted it a bit,' he muttered as Mr Griffiths crouched beside him.

'Let's see if you can put some weight on it,' said the teacher.

Oliver winced at first as he stood up, but then began to hobble away, determined to carry on and refusing the offer of a pain-relieving spray that was being squirted on to Dips' knee by Mr Fisher.

Mr Griffiths gave a little shrug. 'OK, Oliver, try and run it off, but let me know if it hurts too much, right? We can always bring on a sub, if we have to.'

The teachers exchanged a tense smile. 'They like playing the wounded hero, don't they, given half a chance,' remarked Mr Fisher with a chuckle, glancing at his watch. 'Not long to go now, I reckon.'

'Long enough,' grunted Mr Griffiths in response.

There was too. Long enough for College's Yagnesh Sharma to miskick in front of an open goal; long enough for Glendale's substitute, David Nash, to blaze a shot wide – and long enough for Nashy then to drop back into his own area and trip Bax as the number eight was poised to shoot.

Penalty!

As soon as he heard the whistle, Bax bounced back up from the ground. He was keen to get to the ball before Oliver could lay claim to it.

'Oliver!' came the shout from the touchline. 'Are you OK to take it?'

Oliver was still limping slightly and didn't feel entirely confident. Although it wasn't his main kicking foot – his left – that was hurt, it *was* the one that would have to bear his weight as he shot. He looked across towards Mr Griffiths and shook his head as a signal that he didn't fancy the job.

The teacher sighed. 'OK, Iain, all yours,' he shouted. 'Put it away.'

Bax was determined to do exactly that. He was already settling the ball on the spot, ignoring the insults from the nearby Glendale players and even those from the keeper who had not yet retreated to his goal-line.

Crackers had saved a penalty from Bax in the second leg and he was quick to remind him of that fact. 'Not you again,' he sneered. 'You must be a sucker for punishment. You know you can't beat me.'

Normally, Bax would have enjoyed giving the keeper as good as he got, but this was different. He needed to direct all his concentration on to the kick itself. Nothing and nobody was going to be allowed to distract him.

'Back on to your line, keeper,' ordered the referee. 'Save your breath.'

Crackers couldn't resist one final dig. 'I feel sorry for you,' he hissed at Bax. 'The kid who cost his team the County Cup . . .'

Crackers let that awful prospect dangle between them and as Bax ran in, he was aware of a repeated, whispered taunt from his opponent – '. . . miss . . . miss . . .'

Bax had decided to place this penalty in the opposite corner to the previous one, but his heart leapt into his mouth as the goalie threw himself to the right and got a hand to the ball. The power of the kick was such, however, that Crackers could only help it on its way into the net.

'*Goal!*' Bax whooped in sheer relief. 'The equalizer!'

The scorer didn't even bother to torment the beaten goalie to gain his revenge. Bax wheeled away in celebration and it was some seconds before any of his teammates could catch up and smother him with congratulations.

After such high drama, the game continued in almost a state of anti-climax until the referee decided that sufficient injury time had been played. He blew a blast on his whistle to halt play.

'Right, lads, five minutes each-way extra time,' he announced.

Giant only needed another two to put the ball into the back of the same net as his first goal. Sadly for Glendale, having changed ends, this was now the net that they were defending.

Giant had tracked back into his own penalty area to mark Emerson at a corner and as the two of them jumped for the ball together, Giant twisted in the air to try and protect the damaged side of his forehead. He'd intended to head the ball out of play for another corner, but made contact at the wrong angle and glanced it past the gawping Crackers instead.

Giant sat with his head in his hands, not sure what was hurting the most – the lump on his forehead or the pain in his ears from all the complaints of his teammates now that they were 3–2 down.

Glendale spent the rest of extra time virtually camped in the College half of the pitch. Leaving only Bax upfield for nuisance value, Emerson pulled everybody else back to help withstand the siege. And with a little bit of good fortune – as when Kempy's shot grazed a post and the referee refused Glendale's appeals for a penalty – it looked as if they might just do enough to cling on to their precious, slender lead.

Inside the final minute, however, the Blues forced yet another corner and this time everybody – *everybody* – packed themselves in and around the College penalty area. This was do-or-die time. With nothing now to lose, apart from the match if they failed to equalize, even the green-clad Crackers had charged forward to add his height to Glendale's last frenzied assault. Crackers fancied himself as quite a good header of the ball, even though he didn't get many opportunities to prove it.

'If we score now, we can still win this thing on penalties,' he cried out, confident in his own abilities to save one or two in any shoot-out.

'Mark up!' shouted Emerson as Leggy prepared to take an in-swinging corner.

Oliver attached himself to Crackers while Emerson and Giant were locked together as usual. Giant was desperate to make amends for that own goal, whatever the pain. His pride had suffered enough. He made his run towards the far post, while Crackers darted for the near one, leaving other Blues to slot into whatever space they could find as Leggy's corner veered in towards them.

Amazingly, no-one managed to get a head to it. The ball dropped, untouched, into the middle

of the crowded goalmouth and it was a boot
instead that made firm contact. There were so
many bodies in front of Adam that the College
keeper didn't even see whose boot it was . . .

*. . . so whose was it, do you think? Have Glendale
equalized at the last minute? Turn over to find
out what happened . . .*

FINALISTS

. . . we're in the changing room after the match and the contrast is stark – one side of the room is quiet, the other is very boisterous . . .

The raucous song of celebration echoed off the tiled walls.

'We're gonna win the Cup . . . We're gonna win the Cup . . . ee-ay-addio, we're gonna win the Cup . . .'

'Magic! Nobody can stop us now.'

'Apart from Lakeview, that is.'

'Well, yes, apart from them of course.'

The chant changed.

'Champions! Champions! Champions!'

'If that lot don't shut up in a minute, I'm gonna go round there and sort a few of 'em out.'

'If the Destroyer had been here, bet he'd have already done so.'

'Fair's fair – if we'd have been in their shoes, we'd be doing exactly the same thing.'

'*. . . So watch out, Lakeview, cos here we come . . .*'

'Reckon we deserve it, don't you – y'know, in the end. I mean, we *were* the best team over the three games.'

'Course we were – no argument.'

'Bet that poor lot over there wouldn't agree.'

'Who cares?'

'Can't wait till the Final now – when is it?'

'Fortnight's time – end of the month.'

'Wicked!'

'*We are the Champions . . . we are the Champions – of the world!*'

'Huh! Just listen to 'em.'

'Got no choice.'

'*Champions of the world!* Huh! They aren't even *County* Champions yet. Bet Lakeview will stuff 'em.'

'Hope so.'

'Well, dunno – at least if this lot beat Lakeview, we could say we only lost to the Cup-winners. That'd be some consolation.'

'Not much. We ought to be in the Final ourselves.'

The chanting across the room returned to the players' favourite chorus.

'We're gonna win the Cup . . . We're gonna win the Cup . . . ee-ay-addio, we're gonna win the Cup . . .'

'What a goal, that last one – never seen anything like it. There was Sam haring up the pitch after the ball with three of their guys chasing him.'

Sam Lucas grinned. 'Easiest goal I've ever scored.'

'Yeah, thanks to my big boot,' shouted King Kong over the racket going on around them. 'Sailed right over the halfway line. All you had to do was run after the ball and stick it in the back of an empty net.'

'Good job you're a star runner, Sam, or you'd never have made it,' chuckled Kenny. 'Comes with all that cross-country running we do.'

Adam pitched in with another observation. 'Did you see the look on their poor keeper's face when we broke away? He was pig-sick. There he was, stranded up in our area, while the ball ended up in his net again.'

'Don't go feeling sorry for *him*,' Bax muttered. 'He was giving me a right mouthful before I scored that penalty.'

Adam shrugged. 'Well, y'know, goalie's union and all that. I know how he must have felt. Shook hands with him at the end.'

'What did he say?'

'Not a lot. He was too choked.'

Emerson walked past at that point, towel draped over his shoulder, heading for the showers. 'At least their captain wished us good luck when he came up to me after the match. Said he hoped we'd win.'

'Course we will,' boasted King Kong. 'We're the top team in Medland – and we're gonna prove it too.'

'Right,' agreed Bax. 'Lakeview have got no chance.'

Result:	**Westbridge 4 v 2 Glendale**	
	(after extra time)	
	h-t:1 - 1	
	full time:2 - 2	
Scorers:	**Yates, Baxter (pen) Lamb, Taylor**	
	Taylor o.g., Lucas	
Man of the Match**:**	**Emerson Marshall**	

. . . phew! Let's take a time-out with Bax first and then switch attention over to Lakeview and see how they react to the news of their Cup Final opponents . . .

FLOODLIGHT FOCUS

... on **Iain Baxter**

school	Westbridge College
other teams	West Quarter
	River Boys (Emerson's Sunday team)
position	goal scorer!
best foot forward	right
age	11
build	just right for a goal scorer!
nickname	Bax
ambition	to score goals for Scotland
pets	Scottish terrier — just like me!
family	brother & sister
superstitions	score three goals in pre-match shoot-in
hobbies	playing table football
so embarrassing!	missing penalty in Cup semi — first time ever

favourites	
school subject	P.E.
football team	Celtic (& Scotland of course)
book	Christmas soccer annuals
TV programme	soccer highlights — goals!
music	bagpipes! (joke!)
food	porridge! (another joke!)
drink	bottled fizzy water
word/saying	Penalty! — I'll take it!

NEWS TRAVELS FAST

. . . it's Sunday morning and every Lakeview footballer already seems to know who their opponents will be in the County Cup Final . . .

'It's Westbridge!' screamed Joe Vernon, throwing the door of the changing room wide open. 'They won 4–2.'

He was greeted by a mocking chorus from his Sunday League teammates.

'Yeah, yeah, we know.'

'Tell us news, not history.'

Joe looked crestfallen. 'When did you lot find out? Harry's only just been told by somebody. He phoned me up straightaway.'

'We heard yesterday while you went swanning over to Villa Park to watch Jacko play for England,' sneered Ian Coates, who played left-midfield for both the school and Medville Majors.

'England won 4–2 as well,' Joe reported. 'And Jacko scored from the spot.'

''Fraid they all know that too,' said a voice from a corner of the room.

Joe glanced round to see Ben Thorpe grinning at him. The captain's dad had taken the cousins and Elvis to watch their teacher's international debut.

'Already told them how good she was,' Ben admitted.

Joe threw his bag down on to a bench. 'Yeah, right, so don't suppose any of you know-alls will want to hear my other bit of news either.'

'Go on, then, might as well,' Ian chuckled. 'Is it about the Americans putting a man on the Moon?'

'No, it's about the fact that the Wanderers have just arrived in the car park.'

There was a flurry of activity as several players made a dash to the door to try and get a glimpse of the opposition. 'Wonder how many of 'em play for the College too?' cried Elvis.

'Guess we'll soon find out,' said Ben. 'Might've already played against some of them in the Area games.'

'What were the results?' asked Ian.

'East and West both won 2–1 at home.'

'Do you recognize any of 'em?' said Elvis as some of the Wanderers came towards the changing rooms.

Ben shook his head. 'Not sure. Hard to say when they're not in soccer gear.'

'We'll find out soon enough,' said Joe, pulling off his shirt. 'Bet they'll be wanting to check us out too.'

It wasn't long into the game before Dan Cross introduced himself to Ian. The Majors' midfielder made the mistake of trying to beat one player too many on a jinking run – especially when that player was Dan. The full-back left the autograph of his studs down the back of Ian's leg.

'Get up!' Dan snarled as Ian rolled about on the ground in apparent agony. 'Hardly touched yer.'

After Dan received a warning from the referee, the Wanderers were made to pay a heavy price for his foul. Ben lashed the direct free-kick over the defensive wall, past the goalie's despairing dive and into the net.

'One–nil!' whooped the captain, punching the air. 'And there's plenty more where that came from.'

Ben was right. Elvis had a relatively quiet match in goal as the Majors ran out overwhelming 6–1 winners. The main disappointment for the Lakeview contingent was finding out that the scorer of Wanderers' single goal, Sam Lucas, was one of only two College players in the opposition. The other was the bad-tempered full-back who had been sent off midway through the second half following a string of reckless challenges.

'Just glad we won't have to meet that maniac again in the Final,' said Ian, ruefully examining the marks on his leg afterwards. 'Seems he's already banned from the Cup for fighting in the semis.'

'Good riddance,' Ben replied. 'We don't want the Final ruined by some head-case like him. It's gonna be a real feast of football!'

. . . there's still a few loose ends to clear up before the Big Match, so let's start in midweek by seeing whether the East or West Quarter finishes top of the Area league table – many of the Cup Final players are involved in these games too . . .

AREA FOOTBALL

. . . the West hold a three point lead over their Eastern rivals as they play the last round of games, so let's check out who takes the Quarter honours . . .

East v North

It proves to be a seven-goal thriller in Medville, with Lakeview's leading scorer, 'Henry' Tudor, claiming a hat-trick. His third goal clinches East's victory just two minutes from time when he seizes on a defensive slip-up to fire the ball home and put his team 4–3 up.

Despite their success, Ryan Burns of Medville Comprehensive is in a bad mood. 'Bet that won't be good enough,' the goalkeeper grumbles, stuffing his muddy boots straight into his kit bag. 'We needed to win by a much bigger margin today to improve our goal difference.'

Henry jumps at the chance to taunt one of

Lakeview's local rivals, even though Ryan is also the Quarter captain. 'We did score four goals,' Henry reminds him icily. 'Can't help it if you go and let in three at the other end.'

Ryan rises to the bait, as expected. 'Don't shove all the blame on me.'

'All right, let's blame your defence instead. How many Comp players were there at the back today?' Henry smirks, pretending to count their names on his fingers. 'Three out of four, I make it.'

Ryan curls his lip and changes the subject. 'Just hope the County Cup ends up in the West as well. Reckon College will stuff you lot in the Final.'

'No chance!' scoffs Ben Thorpe, the Lakeview captain, who is just on his way back from the showers. 'This is what we're gonna do to them – look!'

Before Ryan can make a move to defend himself, Ben lunges forward and wipes his dirty wet towel in Ryan's face. 'We're gonna rub their noses in it just like this,' Ben cackles.

It's perhaps just as well that the East manager walks into the room at that point. A minute later and he might have found himself having to try and quell a riot.

South v West

There's a late goal here at Shelthorpe, too, where the County Cup Final is due to be played soon. It's scored by the South captain, Matt Eales, on his own school pitch – but unfortunately for the Quarter team, it's also into his own net.

Matt slumps down in the goalmouth, devastated, until the keeper helps him to his feet. 'Just one of them things, Matt,' says Oz generously. 'At least you did score at the other end as well earlier.'

'This end, you mean. That was before half-time. I've gone and scored twice in the same net.'

'Well, just so long as you don't go looking to make it a hat-trick!'

There's no time for any such disaster, but West's single point from the 1–1 draw confirms their status as the new Quarter Champions.

Back in the changing room, Matt puts his personal disappointment to one side and stands up on a bench. 'Which of you lot play for Westbridge?' he calls out towards the West players.

To his amazement, as many as six of the opposition make themselves known. 'Right, come on,' he says. 'Follow me.'

Puzzled, the College captain, Emerson Marshall, leads the group of half-dressed team-mates in the wake of the disappearing blue-shirted figure. They catch up with him in a wide corridor standing in front of a glass cabinet.

'What's this all about?' asks Kenny.

'This!' Matt grins, pointing. 'This is what it's all about – the County Cup!'

There is a collective intake of breath as the College footballers stare at the huge, silver trophy on the centre shelf.

'Wicked!' exclaims Oliver in awe. 'First time I've ever seen it.'

'First time any of us have ever seen it,' laughs Kenny.

'Well, it won't be the last,' says Emerson. 'This beauty's gonna take pride of place in our own cabinet after we've thrashed Lakeview.'

Matt chuckles. 'Don't count on it. I've already shown it to their captain after our game with the East. He took quite a fancy to it as well.'

'Tough! He'll just have to be disappointed, won't he,' replies Emerson. 'The next name on this thing is gonna be ours – I've decided!'

Nobody is going to argue with the captain about that.

FINAL AREA TABLE

	P	W	D	L	F	A	(GD)	Pts
					Goals			
West Quarter	**6**	**3**	**2**	**1**	**12**	**8**	**(+4)**	**11**
East Quarter	6	3	1	2	11	10	(+1)	10
South Quarter	6	2	1	3	9	10	(-1)	7
North Quarter	6	1	2	3	12	16	(-4)	5

FINAL PRACTICE

*... the County Cup Final might be just a few days
away now, but Miss Jackson is still wanting her
Lakeview squad to practise their skills ...*

'Well controlled, Joe,' the coach called out
as she supervised one of the training
groups. 'Now look up and pass.'
Joe picked out a nearby target but struck the
ball more firmly than his cousin was expecting.
Harry managed to get his boot to it, but he was
stretching and the ball bobbled away from him.

'Tighter, Harry,' Miss Jackson demanded. 'Get your body right behind the line of the ball.'

'Huh!' snorted Harry under his breath, wondering whether Joe had made it awkward for him deliberately. 'If he'd put me in trouble like that in a game, I'd have throttled him!'

Miss Jackson moved on to the next group who were working in pairs, trying to keep possession of the ball as their partner challenged for it.

'Well screened, Ben,' she praised the captain. 'Now turn him.'

Dan Maynard was alert to all his friend's tricks – or at least he thought so. He blocked Ben's first two attempts to dodge past him, getting a toe to the ball the second time, but the defender was completely bamboozled by Ben's next nifty piece of footwork.

The captain shaped as if to knock the ball past him but then suddenly dragged it back with the sole of his boot, swivelled and dribbled the ball away, leaving Dan gobsmacked.

'Clever feint, Ben,' said Miss Jackson. 'Where did you learn that?'

He grinned at her cheekily. 'Watching you, miss. Saw you do it playing for England.'

She laughed and reddened slightly. 'Flattery will get you everywhere, Ben Thorpe!'

'Including in the team for the Final, miss?' he said, still grinning.

'Oh, well, I'll have to think about that,' she said, putting on a false frown. 'Might be able to find room for you somewhere, I suppose.'

'On the bench, I hope, miss,' Dan chipped in. 'I could be captain then.'

'Have you decided on the team yet, miss?' Ben asked more seriously.

She shook her head. 'Not quite. I'll have to sleep on it – which I'm afraid is what some people here seemed to be doing on Saturday.'

Miss Jackson was referring to Lakeview's last league game of the season. The teacher had taken the opportunity of resting a number of players, such as the lads who appeared in the midweek area match, but she was still disappointed by the overall performance. Even goalkeeper Gary, a second-half substitute for Elvis, had wasted the chance to stake his claim for a place in the Final. They'd lost 2–1 and his fumbling of the ball over the line near the end cost them dear.

One of the few bright spots for Lakeview had been their excellent goal. Dan carried the ball over the halfway line and as teammates created space for the raiding wing-back with decoy runs,

73

he timed the release of his pass to perfection.

Jaspal Singh, the Blues' number ten, took the ball in his loping stride, shaped as if to try a shot himself and then slipped it inside to Ian Coates who was steaming up in support. Ian had rarely struck the ball so hard, lashing it high into the net past the groping keeper.

The quality of that early goal had proven a false dawn. Nearly all their other efforts, and there weren't that many, had flown wildly astray, consigning Lakeview to their first defeat of the term – not a happy omen for the Final.

Miss Jackson moved on now to where her attackers were still attempting to find their shooting boots. They were setting each other up for different kinds of shots and she was delighted with the one that greeted her arrival. Jaspal's delicate chip looked as if it was going to float over the goalie's head, but Elvis back-pedalled furiously and just managed to tip the ball over the bar.

'Good shot – good save!' she cried. 'Well played, both of you.'

Elvis unwisely tried to show off. 'You have a shot at me, miss, go on,' he challenged her. 'Bet you can't score.'

He tossed the ball out to where Miss Jackson was standing on the edge of the penalty area, not expecting her to respond. He was wrong – and he should have known better. The coach often liked to demonstrate a technique by example rather than words.

She flicked the ball up into the air and everyone – including Elvis – watched it drop and then heard it thwack into the net after her right boot connected fiercely on the volley.

Jaspal sniggered. 'Reckon you might've just lost that bet there, Elvis.'

ADVANCED BALL SKILLS

A skilful player needs to feel comfortable on the ball, able to pass or keep possession with close control even when under pressure. And perhaps sometimes bamboozle markers and excite spectators with a spot of wizardry!

Want to improve your own ball skills? Take a few tips from me.

✓ Screening: keep your body between the ball and opponent – stretch arms out wide and turn sideways to see both him and ball

✓ Feinting: pretend to kick ball but place foot on top of it instead, then roll ball back behind you with sole of foot, turn and dribble away

✓ Passing: (1) volley pass – kick ball with instep before it touches the ground – bend kicking leg and keep ankle firm

✓ Passing: (2) swerve pass – avoid opponent by striking ball left or right of centre with inside or outside of foot

✓ Shooting: (1) chip shot – practise chipping ball over goalkeeper's head into net if he has strayed too far forward off his line

✓ Shooting: (2) overhead shot – if your back is to the goal, jump up and lean back, using non-kicking foot to thrust yourself upwards – then swing kicking foot up higher than ball and kick it back over your shoulder goalwards. Remember to cushion landing with your arms!

✓ Keep practising

GREAT SKILLS!

FIRST THINGS FIRST

. . . There's an important domestic issue for Westbridge to settle first before the County Cup Final. The College players have the luxury of a home match at last – the West Quarter league championship decider against Riverside . . .

The teams are locked at 1–1 with College desperately hanging on to the point they need to clinch the title

CORNER!

How long to go, ref?

Five minutes yet at least.

Robbo, the Riverside captain, urges his team on.

C'mon, team, we've got to score— a draw's no good to us.

Make this one count, Reds.

The ball lands smack on the head of the Reds number nine, leading scorer Joe 'Buzz' Aldrin.

GOAL!

No! Magic save, Adam!

Mr Riley leads the applause from the touchline, both for the header and for the save. The Riverside teacher is also the West Quarter manager and well over half the players in the match are in his Area squad.

Another corner. Keep the pressure on, Reds.

This one's an in-swinger, but Adam leaps high to catch it.

Out, men! Out!

The goalkeeper's long clearance catches Riverside stretched at the back, and two College attackers are on the break against a single defender.

Bax is in the clear.

The captain is soon proven right. Emerson's well-organized defence keeps Riverside at bay – and after the match, he proudly receives the league trophy.

. . . right, time for the Westbridge and Lakeview teachers to name their squads for the Final – wonder which players and formations you might choose? . . .

FINAL TEAMS

LAKEVIEW 3–5–2

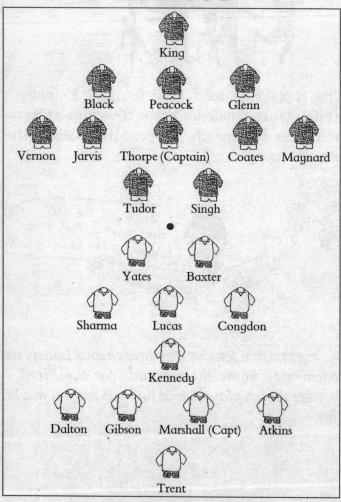

King

Black   Peacock   Glenn

Vernon   Jarvis   Thorpe (Captain)   Coates   Maynard

Tudor   Singh

Yates   Baxter

Sharma   Lucas   Congdon

Kennedy

Dalton   Gibson   Marshall (Capt)   Atkins

Trent

WESTBRIDGE 4–1–3–2

Substitutes:

Lakeview:	Bennett	Freeman	Finch
westbridge:	Roberts	Small	Thornton

Ben Thorpe
CAPTAIN

Emerson Marshall
CAPTAIN

OFF-SIDE!

... for a little light relief before the Final, let's go behind the scenes at the two schools where the captains can give you a guided tour of their changing room to meet some of the characters involved ...

At Lakeview – by Ben Thorpe

One to watch: Steve Jarvis — likes to put itching powder in your kit if he gets the chance

Star potential: Pip Maynard — what's Dan's kid brother doing in here? — he's only five years old (future star!)

Real star: (1)   Jacko — just a pity we can't pick her in the team

Real star: (2)   Elvis — the King — (otherwise known as Michael King)

Top scorer:	'Henry' Tudor — just managing to outscore Ravi Mistry who left before Christmas
Speedster:	Joe Vernon — always the quickest out the classroom when the bell goes
Joker:	Ian Coates — always coming out with stupid jokes — e.g.: how long does a player have to be a half-back before he becomes a full-back? (That's the joke, by the way!)
Misnamed:	Jaspal Singh can't — & James Black isn't — geddit?
Free transfers:	In — Harry Glenn — not wanted by rivals at the Comp Out — Ravi Mistry — still badly missed
Skipper:	Ben Thorpe — Manchester United fanatic, but otherwise he's OK (I think)

At Westbridge by Emerson Marshall

One to watch:	Richard 'King Kong' Congdon – especially when he's coming in to tackle you from behind
Head–case:	Dan Cross – the Hit Man – fortunately banned from Final
Star: (1)	Oliver Yates – told me to put this and nobody's going to argue with Big Ollie
Star: (2)	Adam Trent, our goalie – only cos he promised me a bar of chocolate if I gave him a good write-up in these notes!
Libero:	Kenny's still trying to find out what the word means

Top scorer:	Bax – though not in the County Cup, that's Yaggy
Unsung hero:	Sam Lucas – reckoned he wouldn't even get a mention
Speedster:	Anyone being chased by an angry King Kong
Joker:	King Kong – you have to laugh at his sick jokes – e.g. what's black & white and red all over? A zebra crossing after a man's been squashed by a ten-ton lorry!
Free transfers:	In – Big Ollie – big bonus Out – Dan Cross keeps disappearing
Skipper:	Me! – The Lawman – keeps everyone in order on the pitch (though really prefers playing cricket!)

THE BIG MATCH

LAKEVIEW v WESTBRIDGE

at Shelthorpe Comprehensive School

Saturday 28 March

k.o. 10 a.m.
Referee: Mr. R. Sandford

*. . . OK, so now it's down to the serious business
– the Final of the County Cup – and we've got the
whole match live for you to enjoy . . .*

The game was less than a minute old when
a snapshot from outside the Lakeview
penalty area took a deflection off a
defender's leg. The alert keeper had to dive full
length to turn the ball around the post.

'Great save, Elvis!' cried Harry, helping the
green-clad figure to his feet. 'Thanks – you
rescued me there.'

'Good try, Harry,' joked cousin Joe, running up
to join them. 'You'll do anything to get your name
on the scoresheet again!'

Elvis grinned at them. 'He was just testing my reflexes, that's all.'

The goalkeeper's quick reflexes were called upon once more from the resulting corner. He did extremely well to hang on to a powerful, close-range header from Oliver Yates. If the ball had gone another metre either side of him, even Elvis would have been left helpless.

Lakeview managed to put together a few intricate passing moves to relieve the pressure for a while, though without troubling the College keeper. Their opponents' response was far more direct and only the woodwork saved the Blues from falling behind. Elvis was beaten by a low, skimming effort from Yagnesh, but the ball struck the foot of the post and rebounded to safety.

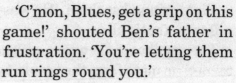

'C'mon, Blues, get a grip on this game!' shouted Ben's father in frustration. 'You're letting them run rings round you.'

The Lakeview captain shot his dad a dirty look. 'Huh! All right for you,' he muttered under his breath. 'I'd like to see you do any better.'

Ben paid far more heed to the next piece of advice he heard. He knew that the giver probably *could* do things much better.

'Try and get the ball out wider, boys – spread the play,' called out Miss Jackson. 'Joe – Dan – push forward more. It's all too tight in the middle.'

The Lakeview wing-backs were always keen to make forward runs, but so far they'd been kept too busy helping in defence. Dan wasn't slow to respond to the coach's encouragement to be more adventurous. When Ian Coates gained possession just inside the Lakeview half, Dan overlapped him and went bombing away up the left wing.

'Coatesy!' Dan shrieked. 'I'm free.'

Not for long. Ian's pass inside a College defender did send the wing-back into the clear, but Dan's fleeting freedom was soon cut short. He never knew what hit him.

CLAANNNGGGG!

King Kong's crunching tackle was like the slamming of a heavy prison door. Dan's world turned upside down. For several seconds, he had no idea where he was – and didn't really care. He lay flat out on the grass, winded, staring up at the clear sky as if he were sunbathing. It was only as he tried to sit up that the pain began, searing up and down his right leg.

While Miss Jackson was administering some basic first aid to her wounded player, the referee gave the College hard-man a stern lecture.

'One more tackle like that, lad, and you'll be off!' he warned.

Miss Jackson decided in the end that Dan was in no fit state to continue. 'I'll have to use a sub,' she told the referee and then called out towards the touchline. 'Will, get that top off – you're coming on.'

Will Freeman tore off his tracksuit top, eager to join in the action. It was his first game in the Cup since Harry's arrival at the school.

'Who's the referee?' asked Mr Underwood as he helped the limping Dan off the pitch. 'He certainly looks the part, wearing all the official gear.'

'He's a local ref – Roger Sandford from Oakfield,' replied Miss Jackson with a grimace. 'He reffed one of my own games recently and disallowed two of our goals.'

'Well I hope he doesn't do that today,' smiled the headteacher. 'I can't remember the last time we scored more than two!'

Ben's free kick was headed firmly away by his opposing captain, Emerson, catching newcomer Will out of position. The ball landed in the space outside the penalty area where Dan might normally have been patrolling and it was picked up by College's Sam Lucas instead. Sam played a one-two with King Kong before releasing the ball into Bax's path as the striker surged forward.

Three touches later and the ball was in the back of the Lakeview net – the third being Bax's clever lob that looped over the advancing Elvis and dipped just below the crossbar.

On the balance of play, it was a well-deserved goal for Westbridge College, but the manner of its coming was somewhat cruel after Dan's injury. The white-shirted players were not bothered about such considerations. They were too busy celebrating.

'Keep your heads up, Blues,' urged Mr Underwood. 'Still plenty of time to get back into this game.'

He was right, of course, but the remainder of the first half followed much the same pattern, with College looking the stronger, more confident side. While Adam idled away the minutes at one end of the pitch, embarassed only by a speculative, long-range effort from Ben that scraped the crossbar, his opposite number suffered two more very anxious moments.

The first was when Elvis had to make a desperate save with his feet from Sam's volley, and the second came just before Yagnesh blasted the ball wide when it looked easier to score. Yagnesh was still shaking his head in disbelief as the referee blew for half-time.

. . . you will no doubt have heard the expression about having a foot in both camps – well let's have an ear in both too and listen to what's being said . . .

HALF TIME

. . . 1–0 down, the dejected Blues gather slowly around an impatient Miss Jackson . . .

'C'mon, boys, hurry up – we haven't got very long,' the coach demanded. 'I know things are not working out the way you probably dreamt they would last night. But there's still time to make those dreams come true – if you really *want* them to . . .'

Miss Jackson suddenly realized there was somebody else listening on the edge of the group – Ravi Mistry. The appearance of their former teammate cheered everyone up immediately.

'Glad you could make it here, Ravi,' she greeted him warmly. 'You're just in time – I hope you've brought your boots!'

Ravi didn't realize that it was a joke at first until the laughter began.

'I've just come to pick up my medal, miss,' he grinned. 'Mr Underwood invited me.'

'Right, you've heard him, the rest of you. You don't want Ravi to have come all this way just to get a losers' medal, do you? So this is what you're going to have to do second half . . .'

. . . over in the College camp, only Yagnesh and Mr Griffiths are not sharing the general upbeat mood . . .

'We've got them on the run,' cried Kenny, splashing water over his head to cool down. 'Only a matter of time before we score again.'

'Sorry about that miss, guys,' Yagnesh said sheepishly.

'Forget it, Yaggy,' grinned Oliver. 'Another goal will kill 'em off, man.'

'Don't get too carried away,' warned Mr Griffiths and then waited until he had everyone's attention – even until the smirk faded from Oliver's face.

The teacher pointed towards where the County Cup sat on a table, glittering in the sunlight. 'Right, see that lovely big silver trophy over there,' he said. 'Well, I want to win it as much as you do, but I'll promise you one thing – so do Lakeview.'

He let that thought seep into his players' minds before continuing. 'You can bet your life that they'll come at you hard for a while and you must be prepared for that, OK? The job's only half done – so you've got to go back out there now and finish it off . . .'

. . . right, all set for the second half – what do you think is going to happen? And who do you really want to win the County Cup? . . .

SECOND HALF

. . . the coaches have had their say and now it's time for the people who really matter – the players – to respond. So let's see who has the Final word . . .

As expected, it was the Blues of Lakeview who made the more positive start to the second half, fired up by their own determination to show everybody how they could really play.

'C'mon, let's win this for Ravi!' cried Ben as they kicked off.

But the Whites of Westbridge were ready for them. Well organized by Emerson at the back, and with sweeper Kenny playing deeper than usual, College were strong enough and good enough to hold Lakeview at bay. The Blues had to be content with shooting from long distance and only Henry gave Adam any cause for concern when his header shaved the bar.

Not that Elvis was totally unemployed. College also kept him on his toes with a couple of dangerous breaks, one of which ended with a low shot from Bax that Elvis had to scramble across his goal to save.

When ten minutes had gone by and Lakeview had been unable to breech the College barrier, the Whites might have been excused for thinking that they had weathered the worst of the storm. So it came as an éven greater shock to the players and their supporters when they were hit by a double fork of lightning.

The first came as a result of a flash of brilliance from the Lakeview captain. Ben demonstrated the same deceptive footwork as revealed in their last practice, only this time he performed it in the heat of battle on the edge of the College penalty area. It was an audacious piece of skill at such a moment and its effect was devastating.

Two defenders were thrown off balance by his trickery, giving him the space he needed for a shot at goal. The ball clunked against the post with Adam beaten, but before the keeper could recover, Ian Coates followed up to tuck the rebound into the net.

'Lovely stuff, Ben!' Miss Jackson called out as her players trotted back for the restart and he gave her a thumbs-up sign. Neither would have believed that he would be repeating the gesture of triumph within a minute.

The equalizing goal had deflated the College players and Lakeview took full advantage of their opponents' temporary distraction. Joe, Steve and Henry linked up together along the right flank and Steve Jarvis's final cross found

Jaspal unmarked near the penalty spot. The Blues' number ten had time to chest the ball down, bring it under control and lash it goalwards before any defender could get in a block. The shot was unstoppable and Adam didn't even make a move to try and do so.

Mr Griffiths was furious at such a sudden reversal of fortune. He strode up and down the touchline in front of the spectators, shouting and gesticulating at his players. 'Wake up! Do you want to win that Cup or not?' he yelled. 'Get stuck in. Show me what you're made of.'

College responded to their teacher's stinging criticism by becoming over-physical, as if seeking revenge for falling behind. They kept the referee busy for the next five minutes or so, committing a series of petty fouls, although King Kong was careful not to incur the official's wrath again. Getting himself sent off was not exactly going to help their cause.

'Push forward, Kenny,' Emerson told the sweeper. 'It's no use you defending now we're two-one down. If we don't score again, we've had it.'

'Cover that kid, Steve,' Ben ordered as Kenny moved up to strengthen the College attack. 'Stay with him.'

The Blues' midfielder took the command to heart. Much to Kenny's irritation, Steve stuck almost as close to him as the number four on the back of his dirt-stained, white shirt. The only kicks Kenny managed to get were the ones aimed at Steve's legs and ankles when the referee wasn't looking.

As the game moved into its closing stages, College became increasingly desperate in their search for the all-important equalizer that might send the Final into extra time. Even Emerson was seen joining in one attack, a rare sight indeed of the captain neglecting his defensive duties.

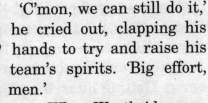

'C'mon, we can still do it,' he cried out, clapping his hands to try and raise his team's spirits. 'Big effort, men.'

When Westbridge won another corner on the right, he waved his fellow defenders forward. 'I'll look after anybody back here,' he told them. 'Go up and show our so-called strikers how to score.'

Lakeview's penalty area became a very crowded place. Although white shirts seemed to outnumber blue ones, it was the goalkeeper's green jersey that rose highest to meet the corner. Hampered by all the other bodies, however, there was no way that Elvis could actually catch the ball. He tried to punch it away, but failed to make the kind of contact he wanted.

The ball ricocheted off his gloved fist and dropped among a group of players around the edge of the area. There was a tremendous scramble for possession and as the ball ran loose, two things happened almost simultaneously.

Sam Lucas drove the stray ball into the net and the referee blew a loud blast on his whistle.

'*Goal!*' cried Sam in delight, but his grin vanished when he saw the referee waving his arms dismissively.

'Sorry, lad – no goal,' Mr Sandford told him, shaking his head as if in genuine sorrow. 'Free-kick to the Blues instead.'

'What for?' demanded Oliver.

'Foul by the Whites' number four on the Blues' number seven,' the referee explained, almost in code. 'Free-kick.'

Mr Sandford had spotted Kenny pulling Steve back by the arm to prevent him clearing the ball and put his whistle to his mouth just as Sam took a whack at goal. Sam was outraged that his equalizer had been wiped off the record, but knew there was no sense in disputing the decision with such a strict referee.

The College players began to take their frustration out on Kenny instead, who was still trying in vain to protest his innocence.

'Why did you have to go and do a stupid thing like that?' complained Sam bitterly. 'Bet you've cost us the game now.'

'You're an idiot!' fumed King Kong. 'This ref misses nothing.'

'Watch out!' cried Bax. 'They've taken the kick.'

Harry's quick thinking almost made College pay dearly for their loss of concentration. He'd lofted the free-kick out to Ian near the left touch-line, catching most of the white shirts out of position, and it was only Emerson's vigilance that came to their rescue. The captain broke up Lakeview's raid himself with a timely interception of Ian's through-ball to Jaspal, but no sooner had Emerson cleared the ball over the halfway line than it was back in College territory again – with fatal consequences.

Joe overlapped up the right wing, racing on to Ben's chipped pass, although it was Henry Tudor's unselfishness that opened up the route to goal. Henry's clever decoy run to the left of the penalty area dragged Emerson wide and created extra space in the middle for others to exploit.

Joe now swapped passes with Steve to evade the challenges of the remaining two defenders and their neat interplay gave Ben a clear sight of goal. This time it was the keeper and not the post that kept Ben's name off the scoresheet. Adam made a tremendous one-handed save, pushing the fierce shot away to one side, but as he scrambled to his feet, the onrushing Joe was first to the ball and poked it past him into the net.

'Magic!' Joe whooped, punching the air before being mobbed by his excited teammates. 'We've won the Cup now for sure.'

When a dispirited College side eventually kicked off again, 3–1 down, they looked resigned to defeat. And little more than a minute later, the referee blew his whistle for the last time to confirm their fate.

Lakeview High School were the new County Champions!

Result:	Lakeview	3 v 1	Westbridge
		h-t:0 – 1	
Scorers:	Coates, Singh		Baxter
	Vernon		

Man of the Match: **Ben Thorpe (Lakeview)**

POSTSCRIPT

. . . scene: presentation ceremony after the match . . .

It was the tradition of the County Cup for the holders to pass the trophy on to the new champions. Shelthorpe School's former coach, Mr Calvert, who now taught at St Wystan's, had been invited back especially to do the honours.

After presenting the College players with their runners-up medals, Mr Calvert patted the large silver Cup for the last time.

'I must be getting careless in my old age, the way I keep letting this thing slip through my grasp,' he said with a rueful smile. 'My Shelthorpe team were knocked out last term by St Wystan's – and when I moved there, the Saints lost to these lads from Lakeview in the semi-finals. So to complete my own hat-trick, I'm now about to hand the Cup over to the East Quarter.'

Mr Calvert finished with what was meant as a joke, but it came across perhaps more as a challenge. 'Look after the Cup well and keep it polished, Blues,' he told them, 'because we shall want it back here in the South next season!'

Ben Thorpe stepped forward to receive the ancient trophy and he held it proudly high in the air to tremendous cheers from the Lakeview supporters. He was followed, one by one, by every member of the first-team squad – including Ravi – to be awarded their individual winners' medals.

Miss Jackson then called all the boys together to pose for a group photograph. 'This is a special one for the family albums,' she announced. 'The County Champions!'

'As long as you come on it too, miss,' laughed Joe. 'The Boss!'

The players jostled happily into position with Miss Jackson persuaded to kneel on the front row next to the captain and the Cup.

'What a fantastic day!' cried Ben as the cameras clicked away.

The teacher agreed. 'It'll be lovely to see this famous old Cup sitting in the school's trophy cabinet for the first time ever.'

'Right, and that's where it's going to stay,' Ben replied with a look of determination. 'Don't care what that chap just said. We're gonna win the Cup again next year as well!'

APPENDIX

RESULTS

SEMI-FINALS

South v East

    1st Leg: St Wystan's 0 v 1 Lakeview
    2nd Leg: Lakeview   2 v 2 St Wystan's

Lakeview won 3–2 on aggregate

West v North

    1st Leg: Westbridge 2 v 1 Glendale
    2nd Leg: Glendale   3 v 2 Westbridge

Teams level 4–4 on aggregate

Play off: **Westbridge** 4 v 2 Glendale

COUNTY CUP FINAL

LAKEVIEW 3 v 1 WESTBRIDGE

COUNTY CUP GOALSCORERS

Winners: **Lakeview**
2 – Mistry, Tudor, Thorpe, Vernon, Singh
1 – Glenn, Peacock, Coates

Runners-up: **Westbridge**
4 – Sharma, Baxter
3 – Yates
2 – Lucas
1 – Congdon, Small, + 1 o.g.

Semi-finalists

St Wystan's
3 – Hira
2 – James, Butler
1 – Varley, Kirk

Glendale
5 – Taylor
4 – Kemp
2 – Green
1 – Khan, Patel, Simpson, Lamb

ABOUT THE AUTHOR

Rob Childs was born and grew up in Derby. His childhood ambition was to become an England cricketer or footballer – preferably both! After university, however, he went into teaching and taught in primary and high schools in Leicestershire, where he now lives. Always interested in school sports, he coached school teams and clubs across a range of sports, and ran area representative teams in football, cricket and athletics.

Recognizing a need for sports fiction for young readers, he decided to have a go at writing such stories himself and now has more than fifty books to his name, including the popular *The Big Match* series, published by Young Corgi Books.

Rob has now left teaching in order to be able to write full-time. Married to Joy, also a writer, Rob has a 'lassie' dog called Laddie and is also a keen photographer.